WITH DRAWN.

For my father, Irving Schwartz, heartfelt son of
New Waterford, who said, We owe everything
to the miners. *JS*

For my father and my son. *SS*

First published in the UK in 2017 by Walker Books Ltd
87 Vauxhall Walk, London SE11 5HJ

This edition published 2018

First published in Canada and in the USA in 2017 by Groundwood Books
128 Sterling Road, Toronto, Ontario MR6 2B7, Canada

2 4 6 8 10 9 7 5 3 1

Text © 2017 Joanne Schwartz
Illustrations © 2017 Sydney Smith

The right of Joanne Schwartz and Sydney Smith to be identified
as the author and illustrator respectively of this work has been asserted by them
in accordance with the Copyright, Designs and Patents Act 1988

The illustrations were done in ink, watercolour and a bit of gouache

Printed in China

British Library Cataloguing in Publication Data:
a catalogue record for this book is available from the British Library

ISBN 978-1-4063-7886-3

www.walker.co.uk

Town Is by the Sea

Joanne Schwartz   pictures by Sydney Smith

WALKER BOOKS
AND SUBSIDIARIES
LONDON · BOSTON · SYDNEY · AUCKLAND

From my house,
I can see the sea.

It goes like this – house, road,
grassy cliff, sea.

And town spreads out,
this way and that.

My father is a miner and he works under the sea,
deep down in the coal mines.

When I wake up, it goes like this…

First I hear the seagulls, then I hear a dog barking,
a car goes by on the shore road, someone slams
a door and shouts good morning.

And, along the road, Lupins and Queen Anne's lace
rustle in the wind.

First thing I see when I look
out the window …

is the sea.

And I know my father is already deep down
under that sea, digging for coal.

When I go out in the morning, it goes like this…

I run out of my house and knock at my
friend's door and we head down
to the old rickety playground.

There are only two swings left now, one for big
kids and one for babies. There used to be four.
One broke, and the other one is wound so high
around the top post it will never come down.

I don't care. I stand in the baby one, and my friend swings on the big one. We go so high butterflies rush through my stomach.

We go so high I can see far out to sea.

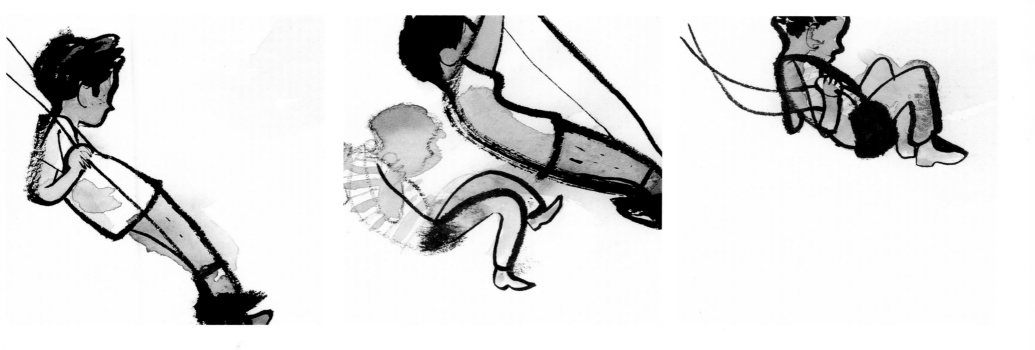

Far out at sea, the waves have white tips.

And deep down under that sea,
my father is digging for coal.

When I get home for lunch, it goes like this…

My mother has a ham sandwich on the table and
a tall glass of milk. I gulp it down and eat
a big pile of carrots.

My mum says, I need your help now.
She sends me to the shop with a list for the grocer.

The shop is only a couple of streets away
on Main Street. The kitchen door
slams on the way out.

Even walking slowly, I get to the shop in no time.

It's so sunny today,

the sea is sparkling.

And deep down under that sea,
my father is digging for coal.

In the afternoon, it goes like this…

I go to the graveyard to visit my grandfather,
my father's father. He was a miner, too.
The air smells like salt. I can taste it on my tongue.

My grandfather used to say,
Bury me facing the sea b'y,
I worked long and hard
underground.

When there are big storms here,
the waves crash against the shore,
battering his gravestone with
salt-soaked spray.

That's OK. My grandfather
is used to storms.

Today the sea is all calm

and quiet.

And deep down under that sea,
my father is digging for coal.

At supper time, it goes like this…

My father comes home from work. He has black
smudges on his face from working the coal. He looks
tired, but he gives me a big smile and a hug. His long
workday is over, and he is home safe and sound.

He showers and puts on clean clothes and comes down
to eat. My mother has been cooking, and the kitchen
smells like chicken stew and potatoes.

I listen to the ball game on the radio
while I set the table.

After dinner, my mother and father sit on
the balcony drinking cups of tea and talking.

The sun sets slowly,

sinking into the sea.

Deep down under that sea is
where my father digs for coal.

At nighttime, it goes like this…

As I fall asleep I can hear the whooshing back
and forth of the waves. I think about the sea,
and I think about my father.

I think about the bright days of summer

and the dark tunnels underground.
One day, it will be my turn.

I'm a miner's son.

In my town, that's the way it goes.

Author's Note

"At the centre of the boy's life in coal towns and villages was the mine. He was raised within sight of it; the smell of coal dust was as familiar to him as the sounds of steam pumps and hoists. The boy may have seen for years his father and older brothers leave for the pit. For most boys raised within these communities, the day arrived when they too surrendered their childhood to it."   (From *Boys in the Pits: Child Labour in Coal Mines* by Robert McIntosh)

If you were a boy in the mining towns of Cape Breton – or, indeed, a child in any mining town in the world – in the late 1800s and early 1900s, you might well have faced the prospect of going to work in the mines at the young age of nine or ten, enduring twelve-hour days in the harsh, dangerous and dark reality underground. Decades later, the life of these towns still revolved around the mines. Even into the 1950s, around the time when this story takes place, boys of high-school age, carrying on the traditions of their fathers and grandfathers, continued to see their future working in the mines.

This was the legacy of a mining town.